SAM LLEWELLYN

THE MAGIC BOATHOUSE

Illustrations by Arthur Robins

WALKER BOOKS
LONDON

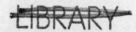

For
Romilly B.
&
Phoebe D.
S.L.

First published 1994 by
Walker Books Ltd, 87 Vauxhall Walk
London SE11 5HJ

Text © 1994 Sam Llewellyn
Illustrations © 1994 Arthur Robins

This book has been typeset in Garamond.

Printed in England by Clays Ltd, St Ives plc

British Library Cataloguing in Publication Data
A catalogue record for this book
is available from the British Library.

ISBN 0-7445-2473-3

CONTENTS

FORGOTTEN ORPHANS

The minibus of the School for
Forgotten Orphans was rambling
down a winding lane in the bottom
of a deep valley, crammed with
forgotten orphans heading for their
holiday.

Joe and his sister Doris were at
the back, as usual. The Fat Ern mob
were at the front, hitting each other.
The Soppy Emmer mob were
behind them, gooing at their dollies.

The reason Joe and Doris were at
the back was that Joe did not like
hitting people unless he had to, so
Fat Ern's mob said he was soppy.
And Doris did not like playing with
dolls, or anyway not all the time, so
Soppy Emmer's mob said she was fat.

There was plenty of noise in the minibus.

"Shurrup!" roared horrible Mr Barge. He was the driver, and the teacher in charge of the holiday.

The Fat Ern mob shurruped. The Soppy Emmer mob shurruped.

Joe and Doris were so excited
they did not even hear.

"You will be punished!"
bellowed Mr Barge,
who hated Joe and
Doris because they
were not evil enough
and they did not fit in.

13

The minibus bounced on in silence. The road stopped. Grey waves were bursting on a rocky beach, their spray splattering an ancient cottage.

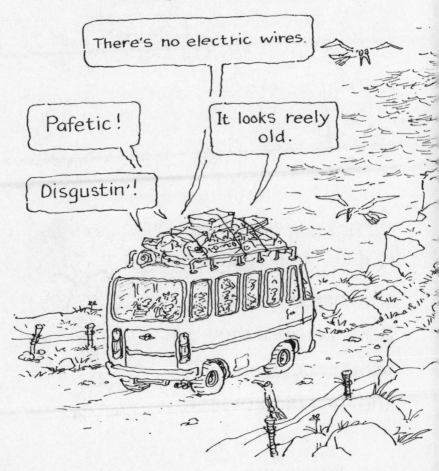

Joe thought it all looked
extremely interesting, but kept his
mouth shut in case the Fat Ern mob
bashed him one.

Doris thought it all looked lovely,
but kept her mouth shut in case the
Soppy Emmer gang made her
change the nappies on their dollies.

The air was full of the cry of gulls.

Fat Ern turned on his ghetto-blaster. Soppy Emmer began to sing along. The racket was huge.

The cottage smelt of paraffin. There were three rooms upstairs.

Fat Ern and his mob looked at Joe. "We're not sleepin' with *'im*," they said.

Soppy Emmer and her gang looked at Doris. "We're not sleepin' with *'er*," they said.

"Quite right," yelled Mr Barge. There was a ladder leading to a trapdoor in the ceiling. "You two can sleep up there," he said.

UP YOU GO!

Up there was a small room with a circular window and two rickety beds.

"I like it up here," said Doris.

"Me too," said Joe. "But don't tell them, or they'll change us."

JOE BLOWS IT

"Right!" roared Mr Barge when they
had all unrolled their sleeping bags
and were downstairs in the
cobwebby sitting-room. "Lovely
nature walk next. Except Joe and
Doris. Joe and Doris, clean up."

"Why?" said Joe.

"Because of not shutting up when *told* to!" yelled Mr Barge.

"That's unfair," said Doris.

"Cheek!" howled Mr Barge, blue in the face. "You're off tomorrow's outing, too. The rest follow me!"

And they filed over the horizon, Fat Ern's mob punching each other, Soppy Emmer's gang plaiting each other's hair.

"Clear up, ho," said Doris. But the cobwebs in the house were thick as knitting.

"Let's start in the garden," said Joe. But the rose bushes were like barbed wire entanglements.

Let's go exploring.

So they walked on to the beach,
where they found a boathouse.

"Must belong to the cottage," said
Doris. "In we go."

In they went.

There were cobwebs, a mouldy lobster pot and a lot of darkness. And hanging on the wall, a thing that looked like a giant ice-cream cone. Joe unhung it.

"Wrong," said a voice. It was an old, slow voice. It nearly made Joe and Doris jump out of their skins. "It's a foghorn."

As their eyes got used to the gloom, Doris and Joe saw an old man.

Then a shadow darkened the doorway: a fat shadow, with no neck. It was Fat Ern.

The old man said, "Blow that horn."

"Blow it yourself, Grandad," said Fat Ern, whose manners were diabolical.

"I'll do it," said Joe, whose manners were fine. He took the foghorn in his hand. It looked old. In fact it looked ancient. He walked outside, on to the beach, and blew.

THE MISTS OF TIME

The horn made a curious sound.
Doris had the idea that it was fading
not so much into the *distance* as
into the *past*. As the last echoes
died, sky and sea turned pearly
grey, and the cliffs and the horizon
disappeared.

"Foghorn," said the old man, cackling. "Brings the fog. And other things."

A noise came out of the fog – a creak and thump, creak and thump, as of many oars. The grey blanket thinned and cleared.

There was a ship in the bay. It had a mast, and oars, and a huge eye painted at its front end.

It swept up to the beach. Men
swarmed down a gangplank.

The old man said, "What do you expect? They're only the Roman Invasion."

One of the Romans clanked up the beach and said something in a foreign language, probably (thought Joe, who owned an excellent encyclopedia) Latin.

"He wants to know for what task you called 'im," said the old man.

Joe thought. "Tidy up the garden, please," he said.

The small soldier clashed his spear across his breastplate.

Orders were shouted.

Someone started a bonfire. In the smoke Joe and Doris could not see exactly what was happening, but it looked like a lot.

In about twenty minutes, the small soldier was back.

"He says the task is finished," said the old man.

The small soldier smiled. Then his dark eyes lit on Fat Ern, and he began to jabber.

"He wants you for a gladiator," said the old man.

Yay! Aw right!

The Roman walked Fat Ern down the beach and up the gangplank. The fog came down again. There was the sound of the oars.

When the fog cleared, the ship was gone.

DORIS BLOWS IT

The cottage's weedy garden and
snaky paths had gone too. Instead,
a straight road of white stone led
to the front door, beside which a
golden oriole was singing in a
bay tree.

"That was quick," said Joe.

"I don't call two thousand years partickler quick," said the old man. "Here's the rest of your lot. See you tomorrow."

Even Mr Barge had to admit that Joe and Doris had done a fair job on the garden. But he still would not let them go on the walk to Hot Sands the next day.

"Tidy up the house," he yelled. "You've only done half the job. By the way, where's Ern?"

"He'll be back in time," said Doris, cleverly.

Mr Barge nodded. Ern would not be missed. In fact his mob was looking a lot happier already.

Thug Ed was making a daisy-chain, and Karl the Killer was teaching a kitten to purr.

"Off we go," roared Mr Barge.

Once the file had gone up the hill
and over the horizon, Doris and Joe
went to the boathouse.

"Nice to see yer," said the old
man. "Tidy the 'ouse, is it?"

Doris nodded.

A shadow crossed the open doorway; a soppy shadow, with ten bows in its pigtails. Soppy Emmer.

"I came *back*," said Soppy Emmer. "My shoe got muddy. Look." On her satin

ballet pump, there was indeed a speck of earth. The old man pointed at the foghorn. He said, "Blow that 'orn."

"Horrid dirty thing!" said Soppy Emmer. "Blow it yourself!"

"Let me," said Doris, who was not fussy. She took the horn in her hand. She walked outside, on to the stony beach, and blew.

A STITCH IN TIME

The horn made its curious sound.
Joe had the idea that it was fading
not so much into the *distance* as
into the *past*. As the last echoes
died, sky and sea turned pearly
grey, and the cliffs and the horizon
disappeared.

"Here they come," said the old man, sniffing.

Doris sniffed too. A powerful smell of cooking was wafting in from the sea. The fog cleared.

There was a ship in the bay. It had a prow like a dragon's head. It shot up to the beach and lay with its sails flapping. People jumped out, and began to wade ashore.

Joe said, "More armour!"

The old man said, "What d'you expect? It's only the Norman Conquest. By the way, there's a tiny catch–"

One of the Norman women trotted up the beach.

She stopped in front of Doris
and said something in a foreign
language, probably (thought
Doris, who shared the excellent
encyclopedia with Joe)
French.

Bonjour, mademoiselle.
Que désirez-vous ?

"She wants to know for what task
you called 'er," said the old man.

Doris thought. "Tidy the house,
please," she said.

The Normans streamed up the beach, down the white road and into the cottage. Clouds of dust began billowing from the windows.

Doris and Joe could not see what was happening, but it looked like a lot. In about twenty minutes, a Norman woman was back.

"Says the task is finished," said the old man.

The Norman woman giggled.
Then she saw Emmer. *"Oo la la!"*
she cried, and began to talk with
great excitement.

Oh les doigts délicats!

"Reckons you'll be red 'ot at
needlework," said the old man.
"Wants you to 'elp with that Bayeux
Tapestry."

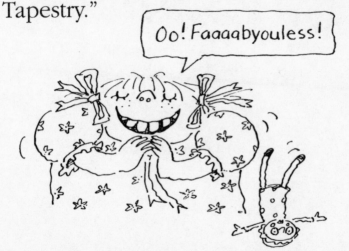

Oo! Faaaabyouless!

The Norman lady walked Soppy Emmer down the beach and boosted her on to the ship. The fog came down again.

When it cleared, the ship was gone.

MR BARGE
BLOWS IT BADLY

The cobwebs and the dust had
gone too. The cottage was scrubbed
clean, and sweet herbs had been
strewn on the flagstones. Two large
saucepans were bubbling on the
kitchen range, sending out delicious
smells.

"That was quick," said Doris.

"I don't call nine hundred and thirty-seven years partickerly quick," said the old man, pocketing a bottle of wine someone had left on the table. "Here's the rest of your lot. See you tomorrow."

Mr Barge sat down and ate a vast supper. Afterwards, he announced that everyone should play close to the cottage the next day. Then he looked about him as if something was missing.

"Where's Emmer?" he howled.

"She's feeling a bit, er, sew-sew," said Joe, cleverly.

Mr Barge nodded and gulped down another glass of wine. Emmer would not be missed. In fact, her gang were looking a lot happier already. Delicate Daphne was wading around in some mud by the river, and Fragile Fiona was arm wrestling Breakable Bella.

So next morning they all stayed around the cottage. In the old days, the air would have been thick with teases and insults. But with Ern and Emmer gone, everyone got on surprisingly well. They even talked to Joe and Doris.

But Mr Barge mooched around with his hands in his pockets, sulking because he had no reason to shout at anybody.

Then he wandered off in the direction of the boathouse.

"Quick!" said Doris and Joe, both at once. "After him!"

They found Mr Barge standing in front of the old man. He was holding the foghorn.

"That there," the old man was saying, "is a foghorn."

IDIOT!

"I know that!" barked Mr Barge.

"It summons fog," said the old man.

"Poppycock!" yelled Mr Barge, delighted to have found someone to shout at. "It is a warning device for seagoing craft in low visibility situations. Look," he bellowed, "one blows it thus." He raised the foghorn to his lips, and blew.

THE KRAKEN
LENDS A HAND

The foghorn blared. Joe and
Doris had the feeling that it was
fading not so much into the
distance as *underwater*. As the
last echo died, sky and sea turned
pearly grey and the cliffs and the
horizon disappeared.

But this time, the echo did not *quite* die. It seemed to hang in the water, and in the rocks underfoot, and to become a huge and awful *bubbling*.

"Here it comes," said the old man, folding his deck-chair.

The fog was cold and full of a powerful smell of rotting fish fingers.

"By the way, there's a tiny catch—"

"What a ghastly smell!" yelled Mr Barge.

54

The old man was well up the beach now. Joe and Doris held hands. Out in the bay the sea was moiling sluggishly, as if a big paddle were stirring it from below.

But nobody ever knew who Mr
Barge thought he was going to
complain to. Because a huge
tentacle snaked out of the water like
the lash of a whip, wrapped itself
round his waist
and flicked
him into a
vast mouth
that had
opened in
the bay.

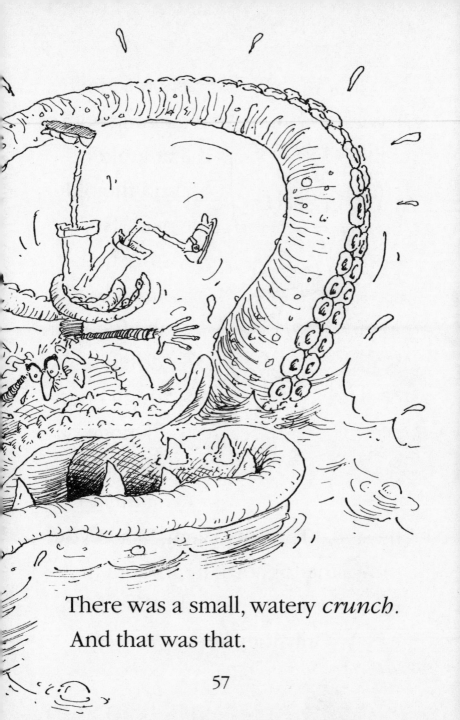

There was a small, watery *crunch*.
And that was that.

Waste of a perfectly good pair of khaki shorts.

"There's no reasoning with that kraken," said the old man. He stretched, and shoved the foghorn down his thigh boot. "Thing you should remember," he said. "That tiny catch. When you blows the foghorn, them from the fog 'as to take one with 'em. I tried to say. Only they kept interruptin'."

The fog came down again.

When it cleared, the water in the bay was still. And the boathouse had gone, and the old man with it. And so had Mr Barge, and of course Fat Ern and Soppy Emmer.

So Joe and Doris
walked back to the other kids
and everyone cheered.
Then they all had a great holiday
which lasted for ever.

Publisher's Note

You have probably noticed some strange words in this book.
That's because they are in Latin or French. Here is a list to help
you understand what they mean.

Latin

Salvete cur clamatis?	Hi. Why are you shouting?
Cotta in fossam incidit!	Cotta has fallen into the ditch!
Ferte scalam!	Bring a ladder!
Horta in tres partes divisa est.	The garden is divided into three parts.

French

Bonjour, mademoiselle. Que désirez-vous?	Hello, miss. Can I help you?
Ugh! Un nid de souris!	Ugh! A mouse's nest!
Eeeah! Cent araignées!	Eek! A hundred spiders!
Oh, les doigts délicats!	Oh, what delicate fingers!